To Keith,
on the occasion of
our shared reading at VPh
~ with warmest wishes,

[signature]

Oct. 2011

Head of a Man

By the same author:

Swinging in Paradise:
The Story of Jazz in Montreal

Who's Who of Jazz in Montreal:
Ragtime to 1970

Head of a Man
John Gilmore

REALITY STREET

Published by
REALITY STREET
63 All Saints Street, Hastings, East Sussex TN34 3BN, UK
www.realitystreet.co.uk

First edition 2011
Copyright © John Gilmore, 2011. All rights reserved.
The front cover shows a detail from "Rizière jeunes plants" by
Jean-Louis Vandevivère
Typesetting & book design by Ken Edwards

Reality Street Narrative Series No 7

Printed & bound in Great Britain by Lightning Source UK Ltd

A catalogue record for this book is available from the British Library

ISBN: 978-1-874400-48-6

For my sister, Sharon

Now, being a man, I could not help consenting.

— Homer / Fitzgerald

One

First, a room. There must be a room. Spare and still. With walls thick to keep the sound out. Some sounds I'll allow. A woman washing clothes by hand in a courtyard. Water splashing in a concrete basin. Sweeping over stone. Women's voices in the distance, in an open space, in a language I do not understand (but not in anger). One car, in the distance, quickly gone. Chopping, even hammering, or a chisel on stone, when it's at the pace of a man's arm, slow and steady and drawn out.

Or, in. Walls thick to keep the sound in, too. A room to go to pieces in, without someone on the other side listening. Like she used to, at night, reading on her bed, her feet elevated on pillows. Reading and tapping on the wall for me to stop. Be still. I am now, or I try to be. I sit motionless at the table. Close doors behind me carefully. Seek out others less and less. (All these years.) This stillness gets me nowhere. There will come a time, I'm sure, when the words will rise and the story be told. But first, a room. There must be a room.

◻

I came to this room on the path that curls up around the rim of the valley. It's the last house on the way out of town. Trees press down the mountainside to the edge of the path, lean there, and sometimes topple. The other side drops away quickly, edges weakened by rain.

◻

The shutter in my room swings out. I unhook it in the morning. It's roughly made: four boards edge-to-edge and a zed holding them in place. The nails are bent over, thick and rusted and pounded in deep. I reach out and pull the shutter closed when it's time to sleep. Many palms have oiled the sill smooth.

◻

There's only a narrow panel of valley I can see from the window, on the left, down below. (If I lean out, then I see more.) Another house blocks the view. A wall of rough planks.

□

It is good to have this room. I have arranged things the way I want them. I have moved the table in front of the window. Not right in front. A little to the right, with space around it. That way, sitting on the straight-back wooden chair, the panel of valley is widest. But the ground drops away quickly beneath the house, and the only part of the valley I can see while seated is the lip on the other side.

□

The bed I haven't moved. It's against the wall, opposite the door. As soon as I come in, I'm beside it. When I lie there in the afternoon, all I can see is the wall of planks next door. There are no windows facing mine.

□

The travellers who come here are young and carry backpacks. The ones who have been travelling a long time are tanned and hard. They arrive every day, on foot, in the late afternoon, dropping heavy loads in the hall outside my door. They come on the bus from the capital. It lets them off in the square. They come to see the valley and the terraces and to escape the lowland heat. They stay a few nights, and then move on.

□

I spend my days here, waiting, the door closed and the shutter open. The room is lit with a dull, grey light that varies in intensity as the clouds thin and shift and congeal overhead. They rarely part. Sometimes I lean out and look up, at the lowness. We are high up here. At night there are no stars.

□

She lets me take water from the kettle, to make myself tea. Tea? Her eyes brighten when I enter the kitchen with my cup. You? I offer, always. She shakes her head, always, laughing, pointing to the deep basin full of muddy clothes they give her to wash. Worrrk. Her drawn-out inflection a playful rebuke. I go back to my room, careful not to spill a drop. She wipes the floor clean every day. I go back to waiting. Later, I hear her singing.

❑

It is my natural state, waiting. Sometimes my waiting is indolent. Sometimes attentive. I am attending on. Preparing myself for. To be ready. Still and ready. I can be. If the room is right.

❑

Every day starts like this. The cracks in the shutter dull. Only her moving. Only us. The water filling. Daylight filling. This short time of hope.

❑

Sometimes, when I awake, I have words. They are given to me in dreams. Francis mantra praying. That was last night. The I's stones. I don't know what they mean, but I like them. I keep them. I wait for more. Sometimes, real dreams, too. Stories.

◻

She sent me ahead. She said she would follow me. But when I arrived, only our luggage was there. I pushed open the door and stepped into a foreign world and went in search of the room that had been assigned to me. (B-something. I don't remember.) I carried the bag across a muddy yard, past low barracks, around wide puddles. (The rain had stopped.) I found my building, and the door at the end of it, and the steps leading up, but the way was blocked by a pool of water. I didn't go in. It didn't matter. I knew what I would find – my room, a cubicle, one among many identical cubicles along a narrow corridor, the others crowded and overflowing, with women in thick skirts and sweaters, and boxes tied with cord and wrapped bundles. Whole families in one small room, eating, talking, feeding children, waiting. Everyone talking in a language I could not understand.

◻

This house has a big room where the travellers sit, on wooden benches, at long wooden tables. Passageways lead out on all sides – to the showers, to the kitchen, to other rooms. And there are large windows with no panes overlooking the valley. Openings everywhere. It's two steps down, to the wash basin and the fire. I go there to get water. Tea? I ask, always. Worrrk, she always answers. And then I turn and step up and cross the big room again and come back here, and close the door. This is my room. I take one step forward and stop beside the chest of drawers. I put the cup down gently on the mat, and open the top drawer carefully (it sticks) and take one tea bag from the torn plastic bag and close the drawer (again, carefully) and lower it by its string. And then I take the cup in the fingertips of both hands and step forward again, three steps, and place it with outstretched arms on the table, on the right, near the back. And I sit. And the dull daylight illuminates the table, and the sounds and odours of life outside come in the window, and they are there. And I am calm to know they are there. The dampened thud of a hoe in wet earth. The trickle of unseen water. I am at rest. A tongue at rest. Waiting.

☐

Her back to me. Always, her back to me, her hands in the deep basin. Always water, running, somewhere. (Over and over, this.)

☐

Once when the door was still open she knocked and stepped inside. Showed surprise. Pleasure. Seeing the room like this for the first time, mine. There was a postcard on the chest of drawers. She stooped, close, then suddenly straightened. My boyfriend! His city! She turned to face me, eyes lit. He say beautiful. Very beautiful. Very cold! Laughs, excited. I go. Husband. How you say? Rubs her ringless finger. Engaged? Engagèd, yes! She looked at the picture again, and smiled deeply, then stood up again and turned and stepped one more step into the room, looking around her. – And me, stepping back, turning too, turning her, by looks and turns myself, spinning circles through a waltz hands clasped arms uplifted spinning circles through a room. But this was slow, and I did not touch her. She stepped into my space and I turned and stepped out, to another space. And again. And again. And all the time I wanted to put my palm on her shoulder the brown sweater a bulb of promise, turn her cupped in my palm until she stood and faced me and both of us finally silent and motionless and the dance over. Nights I wait for her to come back, tap softly on the door with the fingers of one hand.

☐

There are days I wake in this room, I forget why I am here. What it is I am waiting for. The door is unlocked at the front of the house and the bus for the capital leaves every day from the square. But there is this story of which I am a part. The one chosen to wait. And there is this fear. Here is the room, everything as I want. Here, the world seeps in, in increments I can control – the shutter, the door, the exact placement of the chair. Her voice I cannot control, but because I do not understand what she is singing I hear it only as a presence that soothes me. (Her fingers on my temple. The afternoon light.) Over and over the days like this. The sound of water splashing in the basin. Her singing. The others pass quickly in and out, clumping on heavy heels, talking in deep voices (they are almost all men), talking in throaty voices, northern languages. I like it best when it is not my language. Then they are as a brute force passing quickly and gone. They are away all day on trails, and in the evening, in town, drinking beer. Occasionally one stays behind, usually a woman, sleeping or writing postcards by the window. I do not mind. On those days her singing soothes us both.

◻

I cannot explain this. This gazing into absence. I cannot find the words to say what's not there. I can say, robbed. I can say, drugged and robbed. I can say, befriended, betrayed, abandoned in the night. But it's not enough. It's the gaps. I can't see into them. Things rise, but I'm not sure what's real.

◻

I sat up late one night with an old traveller, a solitary man at loose in the world. It was his last night. He had brandy from a stall. We straddled benches in the big room, the long table between us. We sat at the window, looking out. He said he was circling back north after a season on the beaches. (Many pleasures, all a dream.) He talked of a winter retreat, the monastery he was going to, the hard mats they had to sleep on. I tried to explain, but the story would not come clear. (Words again, fallen through.) He said he knew the place they'd taken me. City of angels, he called it. Sailor's rest.

Men wake up there all the time, he said, everything gone. A rain had started, and we watched a single light moving on the other side. He poured again. (Her door was closed). You've got to see it for what it is, he said, nothing more. You were just another gringo. To them you were. Another GI Joe. Fucking Americans, they think they own the world. We clinked cups, bitter pause. The wind came up, a sudden squall, and we slid back along the benches, dragging our cups between us. It's here, he said. The rainy season. Time to go home. He portioned out the last drink and we sat without speaking, listening to the thrumming on the roof. A curtain of water poured off the eave. Then it stopped, just as sudden, and there was only blackness again, and the distant light was gone. He got up to leave. The bench scraped on the floor. Here, he said. He pulled off his sweater. Keep it. You'll need it up here.

☐

(The Lord bless us and keep us.)

☐

Sometimes I think: ledger. The cover black, the spine stiff and stitched and black, too. It opens wide and white and without rules. I make lines across the untouched parts, parallel lines of cumulative impact. Each line elicits a response, in turn another line. Each succinct, spare, efficient. Each indelible, striking, cruel in its calculation. Other pages blot a flood of words, breaking through, rising fast. Unstoppable. And all between the same black covers. A single ledger, to be closed and left on the table at night. The spine aligned with the perpendicular.

◻

Last night there was a bear. It wandered in and out of rooms, and outside again. I could never get the right combination of doors closed, with me on one side and the bear on the other. There was a woman, too. It came up behind her. I told her not to look back.

◻

The table in my room bears the imprint of words. I cannot make them out. A child's first letters. Practiced, pressing. Intaglio. The wood remembering.

◻

And then there are rooms that connect to other rooms, interconnected, arched, endless, with people wandering through. Some rooms are dim, and I don't stop as I move through. I cannot turn to them, offer myself. Momentum propels me on.

◻

(Footfalls.) (Many words.) (Forgotten the rest.)

◻

Wind this morning. And one bark, from below. Just one. It, too, listening. Behind a door. Head cocked.

◻

Waiting to be taken over. That's one way of saying it. The speaking through. The voice of. The done to. This is the room in which I prepare myself. Rituals in solitude. Creases smoothed. Lines aligned. Words rubbed against words.

◻

I eat in my room, the extra towel she gave me spread on the table
for a cloth, the door open behind me. Lately I have taken to leaving it open, just a little. I do not turn when she passes to and from
the other rooms, cleaning, sweeping. But I hear her passing, her
sandals shuffling on the bare wood. I do not look back, but I
think she looks in and sees me sitting here, sees my back, and my
head bent, and my stillness. I hope she sees my stillness.

◻

I am a poor host. I should step into the hall when I hear her
passing and insist. Lead her in and seat her in my chair, at the
table, and take her pail from her hand and put it to one side,
and there, gesturing, I want you to, please, put the plate of nuts
and biscuits before her on the cloth and touch her lightly on her
shoulder, just with the tips of my fingers, on the plait of her
sweater, so lightly perhaps her skin will not register my touch,
and laugh (we would both laugh), time for lunch in Canada.
And I would touch her again with a different meaning this time,
stay, don't get up, and then hurry to the kitchen and pour
another cup from the kettle and bring it to her. Tea. Your tea.
And I would take my cup and sit on the bed, on the foot of the
bed (the covers are straightened and pulled tight and neat, I
make it carefully every morning she can see it in passing a man
who keeps his room neat) and I would laugh and gesture again

and show her again leaning over reaching out taking a nut for myself and a biscuit.

□

Though it is only just after noon, I want to sleep again. Close the door and lie on the bed. Close the shutter, too. Extinguish consciousness. This is my consciousness, this extinguishing. The going down into darkness. (The story, after all.) But this darkness is more than sleep. She is not in the next room, sleeping lightly, not there to come to me in the dark quickly when I cry out. This darkness is the going down darkness, the obliteration of time darkness, the pinned under fathoms darkness, the end of all motion darkness. Here there is no waking to an urge or a touch. Here the door is bolted, the glass of water by the bed untouched. From here, one does not come back with stories to tell. From this one does not awaken in wonderment. From this, one returns with nothing. Only dread.

□

Beautiful dreamer, dream unto me.

□

Here is one beginning. I am thirsty for revenge. The brown river is dry. The river bed has cracked and curled and shrunk, the way paper curls and convulses on the log an instant before it ignites. I walked the streets of the capital like that, dry inside, tasting the need, the thing craved, the absence of it.

□

Here is another. There I went out a thousand tides ago, in a warring time, on a cresting surge. A storm lay upon the sea and the isles, and the river was in full flood when I landed.

□

Not in this room. Far away. She can be a stranger, or we meet as strangers and this becomes our friendship. She seats me on a hard wooden chair as soon as I come in, and ties my hands behind the chair. Then she lies on the low bed before me, undraping herself, languorous, showing me, watching me. It thrills her.

☐

Or, I let myself in, and slouch into a deep armchair, and hook one leg over the arm. She comes in and sits down across from me, on the sofa. She removes nothing, only parts her thighs a little and presses with her fingertips under her skirt. I can see nothing of her body but her bare arms, and her long, white neck when her head falls back, her mouth open, convulsing.

☐

Today she came to me of her own accord, knocking at the open door behind me. (Leaves, suddenly airborne.) I turned on my chair and met her eyes, meeting mine, a moment only. Then she looked down and smiled and her head dipped almost imperceptibly, settling into the space left by her falling breath. (Something inside me has been made visible now. I cannot call it back. It is done, my coming here.) One step into the room and her two arms rose with her next breath, lifting a clean white cup towards me. Tea? Her eyes rose with the rise in her voice. And she looked at me again, hesitating, then stepped again, once more towards me, standing before me now, her arms still offering, as I stood up. And it was my turn now to avert my eyes, looking down, taking the weight of the cup lightly on my fingertips, our fingertips touching an instant before she let go. This simple act. Thank you. Thank you, nodding. Relieved, she stepped back, one step, out of the space we had shared, then turned in silence and regained the door. There she turned again, sure now. Big room. No people. I finish clean. Beautiful, yes? You sit? Look? Thank you, nodding again. Thank you, turning where I stood, my feet fixed, turning with my arms still raised in front of me, holding the cup, turning towards the small table. Here is good for me. But thank you. Here is good. You sit? I indicated the chair, pushed away from the table by my rising, the angle of it open. You sit? She smiled and shook her head quickly, just once. Left quickly by the open door.

□

That which stalks me circles me, seeking flesh, stepping into the space I step out of. My hand finds my own flesh, a comma. (You are a flower, I said, kneeling. A flower, beaded.) But not this morning. This morning I am the hunted and the hunter. I am the tiger. I am the destruction and the night. Her eyes lowered, waiting, holding forth the cup. Make no mistake. I am the tiger. She steps forward. I am the claw.

□

She is singing again. It is long past the hour I go to her for water and the house is still except for her singing and the splashing in the basin. I want her to go away today. I cannot live in her house today. I cannot bear the sounds she makes today, the closing of a door, the shifting of a bench. She is waiting. She knows I am here. (You have the silence I am guarding for you. You have my caution and my caring.)

□

(She followed me here. As the story followed.)

□

Curled with my curl, belly to my back, she rose and left in silence, went back to the basin in the mid-afternoon light and we were alone like that, in the house, alone. She-sounds, gentle she-sounds, rushing water, and me waking into the stillness, alone. Then rises my claw she is gone. Then rises my claw she comes to me again, and again she slips beside me silently murmuring stifling me murmuring to accept me.

□

I do not want this woman beside me take her away. Take away these voices one voice after another voice. (And mine eyes. And mine eyes.) And good there is a wall, and a headwall, too. This the embrace, into this will I empty. Out of chaos, eros. Out of eros, voice. My resurrection is my word, but my story is shattered, my root blasted, my tongue torn. This going down go down – the incantation of forgotten words. My song is no song till she sings it.

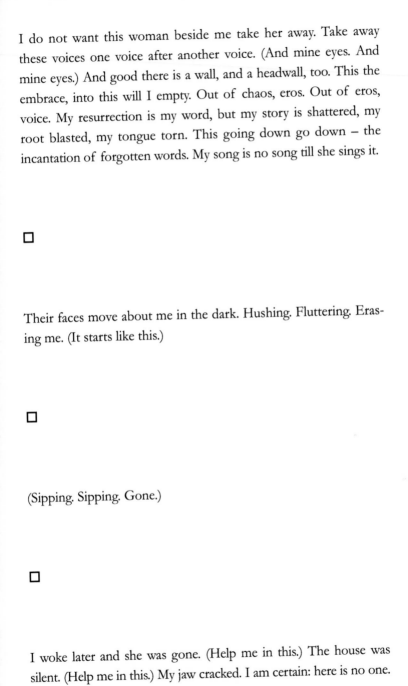

Their faces move about me in the dark. Hushing. Fluttering. Erasing me. (It starts like this.)

(Sipping. Sipping. Gone.)

I woke later and she was gone. (Help me in this.) The house was silent. (Help me in this.) My jaw cracked. I am certain: here is no one.

☐

The room was lower. (Dream the dream on.) They gave me this room. (Dream the dream on.) Here you will sleep. Don't worry. No one.

☐

Always these voices, always. Hovering, in shadows, waiting. As I wait, to be given.

☐

Darkness comes early here. The valley fills with darkness, dripping in. Sounds drown. (An insect giving up.) Now is the time. The smell of cooking on her sleeve. The glow of fire on her skin.

☐

She is there. (Breaths.) (In sedges.) (Waist deep.) (In moonlight.)

□

Something is moving, circling where I cannot see it. (Not far.) I register everything as it was. The door. The window. My jeans limp beside the bed. The sticky heat rising. Their voices rising, softly, beyond the door.

□

This I know: They were waiting, all of them, waiting. Seated around the table. They looked up as I came out of the room. (Action!) The old woman rose and went to the stove, and stirred the milk. The boy was in the same place, at the table, resting on an outstretched arm, a cautious smile, watching her. All eyes watched her. Come. Sit. You are tired. We don't want wake you. (Water splashing in a basin.) The bowl is waiting at my place. There is bread in the basket. She speaks again. We finish, but we wait for you. Come, sit. Drink.

□

(Come back.)

◻

I immobile. Lying on my bed. Watching the light fade, the darkness grow. Listening to them coming back, stamping mud off, recounting adventures. Listening to her working, a pot scraping on the steel flange. Her hands in running water. A body, too, (faint), in the shower, slaps of water hitting the floor. Then footfalls, whispering. Doors closing, extinguishing. Then stillness. Darkness. I immobile. Forgotten. Left. Unnoticed. (Please don't.)

◻

Sometimes an impulse so strong it leaves the blank skin trembling. These walls are not thick enough. I turn in, shredded. Words rub against words. Dry rasp.

◻

She didn't knock. She slipped in alone and shook me. Time to go. You sleep all day. You very tired. We don't want wake you. We go now. The car is waiting. They were talking, moving to and fro, making preparations, hurrying. Looking in at me as they passed. She was right, the night air was cooler. A good time to travel.

□

There is no edge, no border to step over into trespass. There is only the blunt, dull weight of darkness. You step into it, and down.

Two

No going back. One room after another until here: the bus silent in the square, the long walk up the path, the shutter swung open. Now, wait. The day in the vacant field grows long. The day under the briars. There, on the dry packed earth, the birds above me in the thickets, the long thorns that dimple flesh. There I lay, quiet on the earth, waiting to be found.

◻

There is only the waiting. Rise. Lean out. Look up. A motionless, monochrome sky. Below, pools, figurines moving. Dark, indistinguishable, treading narrow paths. As we begin. As it was. World without end.

□

She is singing again. Love. My heart. I don't remember the rest. Miss you. Something more. When she stops I still hear it. Absent song. Finch, on a wire. Gone.

□

I remember a valley I stopped in once, the village square, the road out to the fields. There was water trickling in stone-lined channels, and a house under a bower. (The hot dry stillness beyond.) I look at postcards. The eucalyptus, the cooing of doves.

□

Always gone. Always absence. (Falling away.)

□

Each day I come back to this room, carrying water. Ready, I think. And then, nothing.

□

There was a couple, living in a house. She took me to them. I watched them. The woman wore her hair in braids, pinned up, and her face was soft and kind and her hips full and reassuring. The man had rich brown hair and a wisp of beard, and he was telling a story, walking around the kitchen telling an elaborate story. He hesitated sometimes and seemed to lose his way, but she was patient, and smiled at him, gentle and knowing, and after a long, unhurried silence, he began again.

□

Something more is expected of me. Shift. Motion. Confession. A giving up, of something. I have been holding myself too long. Holding too long my waste breath. (Imagine the extraction.)

□

The rigid chair waits at the table.

☐

The form observed. The deliberate measured motion. Anticipating. Rising. Being there first. Anticipating her turning, this way and that, her face turning away. The thick rearrangement of clothes.

☐

Surfaces scored. Rapture annihilated. Incantations. Repeat after me. (No. Never.) My will be done.

☐

Feeling always: this is tonic, the pull of tonic, towards the tonic. Towards which every lapsed vigilance. (Birch.)

☐

The repeated no never. Words in motion. Anticipation. Motion again. The pebbled skin. The sudden lash. The hushed voice.

☐

The lines precise now. Pure. Each syllable clipped. Over and over. (Ribs. A succession of swells. Slow rocking under a blue summer sky.)

☐

Into the day she walks free. It is I bound.

☐

This morning, before dawn, I woke suddenly to the sound of my name. I went to the shutter. Wet earth. Cold drops. (Her wet black hair.) The house was still. I lay down again, alert, listening. Waiting to be called again.

☐

She is there, and I am here, and it is good that she is there.

□

Those artists that never still the hand. (The compass point, swinging.) Keep moving. Always, moving. When the hand is moving. By this you will know me. (And by this.)

□

The slow mounting, yes. But I cannot imagine the coming apart. Not the full giving over to it.

□

She is singing again. Falta. Falta de amor. A succession of stammers.

□

I need this one assurance. That she watches over me. (It starts again.) That she sits on her stool, short, soft, indolent, her smooth, bare thighs crossed high. Watching over me. Watching a man slouched in the doorway, looking out. (She no come back, Joe.)

☐

Only the darkness between them. I am not stirring between them. I am in this doorway, waiting. The line will not pull free.

☐

Circling this absence. Always this absence. Looking after her (absence). Days like this, looking out. Behind me, she waits, baby-skinned. Behind me, the room of shouting sailors. I was deposited here. Washed up. Alluvial. (Unknown shores.) She watches over me, watches me swaying, looking out. (To sea.) (To sea.)

☐

But if across this I draw a sheet. The wash of sleep under afternoon light. And the swelling of hips held close. Listen, the silent flow. The slow rocking. (Soon, she rises.)

□

Aureola. Ring of desire. (She must have a name.)

□

I cannot reach down and take her hand. Imagination is not being permitted me here. Something resists.

□

I stop and listen to her song. I turn and look at the door she came through. I see her there, her downcast eyes, her gift extended. The weight of all this on me. I close the shutter, lie back on the bed. Not today, the darkness. Not today, the tangled line.

□

I wake from different rooms, always into the emptiness of this room.

◻

It is the soft expanse of warmth I crave now, warming me like summer dunes. (The lines are faint.) Her volume the talisman, the polished stone where water pillows. And the warm pale slope, suspended in light. (A field of orange.) I move over the expanse of her, her belly rising like a slow flood beneath me.

◻

Dyes bleed. Pressure foments. Words crack. (Fish the seams.)

◻

She lies down some afternoons, before the bus stops in the square and the travellers come up the hill. Sometimes I hear a radio in there with her, when I go to take water from the kettle. I'm sure she does not undress. She lies on her back, her sandals off, one arm draped on her belly, or stretched above her head. Listening. The water I take from the kettle is sweetened by the knowledge that she is listening. I put the kettle back carefully. Alone with her in the house.

□

(Pool to pool. The free flow.)

□

I think she would welcome me, but I cannot go. (Only hold her, between my hands, softly, her soft skull. Occupy her. The long drawn-back sheath. The girder. The rain about us. This would be rest.)

□

I hear the exclamation, but it is not mine.

□

(The repeated no never.)

◻

Not one line recalled.

◻

Nights I take up vigil. I sit facing the bed and the wall behind. The blanket is pulled tight. The shutter is still open. The creaking of the floorboards stops. Bodies lie still, suspended. Around the black void of the valley, suspended. Bodies at rest. Mute. Stirring on mats. Somewhere a hand reaches through netting. I listen into the silence. The stirrings. The deep grass pushed aside. (The moment of death.) In this vigil is my salvation. I must persist. I know no other way.

◻

But to get back to this idea of confession. Yes. (Cold water first.)

◻

Bare the flesh, there the story. Can't say can't say can't say.

◻

Bear charges into the clearing. Voices echo round the cirque. (So I said to her.) Blooms in the high meadow. Lone wolf. And on the lake, one merganser, all night. Must be fish.

◻

The drift of her voice turns me, softer than a hand.

◻

Currents abrading. I can no longer control this. The more I try to fashion. (Discipline. Yes. Is pleasure. Yes.) The lines rehearsed. Over and over. A soft voice, explaining. (Someone else's creation.) Octave, sestet, coupled. Speak low words, mother. May I, should I, can I. (Mother, may I take a step?)

◻

(I go. How you say?)

◻

I will bring her. When everyone else is gone. Show her. (What leaning out can do.) The shutter open. Night in the valley. Flickers below. Water flowing, close by. This night, it starts. I insist. Look down.

◻

Some ways the hand has: cupped, circling, singeing. This that is offered. The expanse of skin. The creature's dimensions. The house alone. (The curtain drawn aside.)

◻

Halves pried. Permission. To be attached so firmly as to. This first. Never giving up, that's what she said. Never surrendering. (Make her.) This part over and over.

☐

Forgive us this, our daily.

☐

(Our sins.)

☐

Grace. Declension. World without end.

☐

It is their voices that please me. Their soft way of approaching. Their way of yielding. Folding. Around the thrust. A weight of darkness, taken back. My buttocks clutched. The reassurance, even insistence: we are not fragile in this. From all corners folded. Stone in velvet.

□

(This would be rest.)

□

She is singing again. The old words. Refrains turned. Burr and line.

□

Sometimes there is no one there. There is nothing beyond the wall. Only the fractured silence, stretched taut. (Skin taut, too.) Held that way. (This a bowl, this a mound.)

◻

I dreamt failure last night. Failure, and the unavoidable conse-
quences. I fell back to sleep and dreamt again. I was looking for a
word. Creation. (The book held full in the palm.) I could not find
it. The more I looked, the more the words tumbled out of order,
until order itself collapsed, and creation was nowhere to be found.

◻

(Soft is OK, she said.) (Give me licence. Where I want. What I want.)
(We used to read poetry, aloud. To each other.) (You need someone
to be unreasonable with you. You take far too many liberties.)

◻

Her way of crying out. (Any number of reasons.)

◻

These sudden impulses of words. The pushing of one plosive, the ejaculation of one word – and the rest is lost. Complete utterances, lost. What's left: the over-stimulated nerve. The raw exhaustion. The crumpled, curled silence.

□

Not now, the knowledge. And the worst of it, never. Never the experience. Only the meaning.

□

Fin, no, the circle. Fin, no, the story again.

Three

(Dream the dream on.)

☐

Hand-held. Tipsy. Follow her.

☐

Her palm cool pumice. Tugging. (Left.) (Left right.) She took something, said something, took another. Pulled again. No worry, Joe. I care you, Joe. You happy. You like. (Water rising. Taking its course.) We crossed an open straight. Billows above. (Something free.) Sweeps of sea-breath. Sail and thwart. Polestar! Pulling me on, pulling me on. My flat step slap step, her prow purpose. Here. Here, Joe. Such a little hand. Such small, insurmountable barriers.

□

(Stand. Just stand.) We here, Joe. No worry, Joe. (Stand.) Rings around the knot, the grain showing. (Stand.) Softness against me fragrance against me swelling against me breath.

□

I hold you, Joe. You OK, Joe. I care you, Joe. (Stand. Just stand.) O rigid snag, swaying. To sea! To sea!

□

Hold to! Sea wash! (Stand.) Her faint weight shoring me. (Stand.) Cheek and palm, pressing me. (Stand.) Marked and inked and pressed upon. Whole generations, numbly to sea.

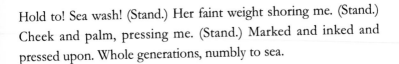

Earth, from her, rising. (Whisk.) Soil. (Whisk.) Damned and rising. Away! Her eyes, rising. (Say nothing!) Red glow. (Nothing!) (Breathe.) (Breathe.) Earth, from her, rising. Away!

Hard ahead. (She no come back, Joe.) Hard ahead. (Breathe!) She lowered her face, pressed me again, relinquished. (My shirt, sticking.) She clutched my arms, my elbows, took my wrists. Waltzed me gently. (Cracked a tiny seed, a nubbed brown grain.) Ice, calving. She felt it. Dug in. Tugged sharp. (Joe!) I fell free and hard, unbolted, pitched to the foam and whipped through to my stone skull, submerging. Sea bed. She followed me down, a wet tent, raining billows, laughing. You heavy, Joe! I no hold you, Joe! Lips to my ear. The tent of her settling. (Settling.) Fingers pry my skull from the wall. (Meadow. Breeze.) (Moss.) (A rustle.) You head, Joe. You head OK, Joe? Cupping me. Spilling over me. Nepenthe. A bead, squeezed. A seed, pursed. (Language).

◻

The frail bones of her cradle. Too far to reach. (Dark sky.) Sea swell, her sea swell, her palms, her little fingers. (Joe?) (You OK, Joe?) (You want I get help, Joe?) Little brown. Little fingers. Where are your eyes? Skull's cavity. Blank. Furrow. Little brown, cradle me. All I can do. (Joe?) All I can do.

◻

Black face, little black face, where are your eyes? (Joe?) Hood the black hood the black earth the glacial milk. (Joe?) Black speaks black moves black face north face. (Joe?) Moon behind Temple. (Joe?) All I can do.

◻

That was one way.

◻

A faint hint of sunrise on her skin. (Imprimatura.) Black closes. The chord slips through. (All hands!) Slips free. Adrift. A phantom, blacked. This I know. This.

□

Summer will come, I'm sure. Her brown washing me. (The slant shaft, remember?) Polaris. Impulse. The unfolding comma. (What, Joe?) If I. Could reach. That field. Of brown. (Figures passing, through trees.) Little brown. Brown wash. Waiting. Far side of the moon. It's there. Say the word. (Say the word, mother.) Say the word.

□

Where the eyes, stars. The lee shore. Tiny, warm fingers. Remember me. Remember me.

□

Joe? You speak, Joe? You thirsty, Joe? I get coca. You drink. Coca. Make you strong. OK? I go, fast fast. You stay, OK? OK, Joe? You stay.

◻

Light. Rosy-fingered.

◻

Spars, lifting and falling. (Her lee. Her lee.)

◻

Scratch out any hint of pity. Hard and spare. Drawing them out till they're taut. An even number. Count 'em.

◻

(The bush goes back for miles. Pipits. Boulders and bowls. High totem, split. A confusion of nests and rings.)

□

By the brave. Bring her in. Thighs bunched. (Claw.)

□

Pour. From one flat bowl to another.

□

Here. Like this. Green spring shoots, sliced through. (White.) A mountain of cushions. At four the sun dropped low the strait glowed blue and burnt. Wind flicked. Through deep snow I drove her forward. Sonatine. Sonnez les matines. Bracelets rang on her wrists. Cuts to the air and sheen, the pale gauze rent. (Orion.)

□

Bound in roan. The whole mass of torso racked lean. Spars unbending. The body must.

□

(Thank you, sir.) The bond the bolt of cloth the thorn-pressed dimple. Mound. I find tresses. (Like this?) Let down. (Whisk.) The whole shorn rise whisked clean and rustling. Tall seed grass, rustling. Omni. Omni Déo.

□

Measure this out. The bearable and the unbearable. Soon fall. Soon relapse. Soon release.

□

(Joe?) (I here, Joe.) Rosy-fingered. Salt-licked. Crystal. Her brown cradle over me again, her scent. (Joe?) Arched. Reaching. Do not deny me this. Little brown. Little brown. Auburn and fire.

□

(We have just received your lovely card. Seven weeks to get here! Thank you for thinking of us. We are all well, except for Maddie, who has the sniffles.)

☐

(Joe?) What hands, what faint tips, buds for my lips (a seed grows there). Care for me. Let me hold you. O god let me hold you let your hair fall down around me tent of stars.

☐

(Cottonwoods fluttering. Night comes on the river.) (The long walk back.)

☐

Waves. Shingle. Wash. (Joe?) Never leave me. (Joe?) If I. Could lift. One hand.

☐

(Drink, Joe.) Black. Black river. (Drink, Joe. Give you strong.)

☐

Black speaks. Black gathers.

☐

(Joe?) Now I see. (Joe? You want I get more?) – No. Thank-you. She exhales laughter. Giddy. Dabs my face with kisses. Dry, cool. Child's play. (Bathe me mother take all of this up off me.) Breath again, wind, my own deep sigh. My neck, lips. (I worry you, Joe.) Puppy nose. Tongue tip. Weight upon me her weight upon me. Blanket of stars.

☐

The night. The sea still running.

□

She hears it. The room behind us. She hears it. Love's old sweet song. (Aie, Joe!)

□

She like, Joe. She tell me. She like. Not all man. Special man. She like this man. He come here many time. Always take her and she happy happy! She love him! She tell me. She love him. She happy. I know. She my friend. She tell me.

□

You know this man. I see you talk him. You no remember? He say you stay. You want go. You very drunk. Bad drunk. I look you. You no see me, but I look you. He talk you, he say stay. I happy you stay. I like you, Joe. I care you. See! You strong now! You listen me now. No before. Before you no listen. I afraid. Very worry. I like you, Joe. You want I get drink, Joe? OK, I no go. I stay. Like this. Like this, Joe. I stay. I know. You like, Joe. I know. I know.

☐

You soft skin, Joe. Like baby.

☐

Aie! He do again! You listen, Joe? Soon. I know. Soon come. Strong strong. You listen. You like listen, Joe? Me, too, Joe. Me like, too. With you. Aie! I think special tonight. Tomorrow maybe he go. He sailor. He go far. Always come back. One month, two month. Always come back.

☐

I like, too, Joe. I like here, with you, like now. Listen. You good man, Joe. I like you. I like kiss you. You soft skin! I like listen with you. Make you strong. I know. I care you, Joe. Make you happy. Yes? Aie, he do again. My friend crazy tonight. I know. Very crazy. You listen, Joe? You like girl crazy, Joe? I like, Joe. I like. Sometime, listen my friend, I go crazy. You like, Joe? You say me, Joe. What you like, you say me, OK? I care you, Joe. I no go, Joe. I you girl. You want, Joe? You say me what you want, OK, Joe? Joe? (Joe?)

◻

Compass, quivering. The arrow, quivering. Floating over me. Long straight. Long slope. Bare slope. True north.

◻

Sometime I come here, no man. Just me. Just listen. Boss no find me. My friend – she – she know I here. Sometime she find me.

◻

Sometime she come here, too. Listen. She, me, together. But I like just me. I make special key, secret, just me. Other girls, they know. They no bring man here. They know my room. They good. Sometime they open door. You OK, Baby? They care me.

◻

(Twenty torsos, after female torso, unknown.) (Arms pinned.)

■

Sometime, all I want, sleep. Sometime listen. I like listen, just me. Just listen. – No, Joe, you OK. No problem. No problem, Joe. I like you stay here. I care you. I know you. You like listen. We same same.

■

Sometime quiet, very quiet. I no listen man. Only girl. Sometime laugh. Sometime come. Sometime I listen door. I no know – who? Many door here, many people. My friend I know. When she with special man, man tonight, I know. Always crazy. You listen, you know. Sometime I listen, I like. Sometime I sad. I want finish. I no want crazy, just quiet. Listen quiet.

■

Here, me alone, yes, but people, they everywhere. Always people. I like listen people. I like listen talk. Quiet talk. No shout. I like listen come – beautiful, yes? – very beautiful. Special secret. Every person have special secret. Very special. I like this. I like listen men come. Yes, I like! Like animal, die. Like everything finish. No more war. You understand, Joe? Beautiful. Very beautiful, but sometime very sad. Lonely. Men, they baby. They afraid, Joe. I know. Even strong come, even crazy sex. I listen. I know. They afraid. They want strong, always strong. But I think afraid. Lonely afraid.

❑

Some girl they no like men come. Too strong. Too crazy. I listen. I think no strong. I think afraid. Like baby. I know. I listen.

❑

Pulse. The weight of one small egg.

❑

You no want listen, now. I know, Joe. I know. Sometime I no want listen, too.

□

Give us this day. The stars gone. The boy shouldering crates through the courtyard. Women going room to room, sweeping water to drains, laughing. Whispering. They know. Both sides, listening. Amôres.

□

Soon I go, Joe. You no want me go. I know. I feel you, Joe. I like you. We together. My room. Secret room. You room, too, Joe.

□

(Girls bring us food and drink and bathe us. Clean robes, too. And then the door pulled closed again, leaving us alone and robed in darkness.)

□

All hollow. All hallowed. Banked between. The first cradle, held. Continuous, hard-forming, the long approach. The long expanse of skin. Breath. From distant calls the spire announces: Here is gravity here is mass here is den. Coaxed ridges, crumbling. Anointment. Incense of ferment. Cincture, girdle, calf. A swaddle of thighs.

□

Voices wheel round us the whole dark night, murmur one last time, and vanish.

□

(Many hearts.) (Many words.) (Forgotten the rest.)

□

Then say, this happened. In cavity, down passageway, crossing court. A succession of closed doors. Sailors shouted, girls squealed. (A cracked vase. Split pod.) I could have said, turn here. And again, here. I could have said, this door, open this door. I could have. But what is there now, but six paces, and an open shutter, and the earth falling away.

☐

Certain kinds of motion belong here. Nothing more. One follows, one leads. Turn sharp by the open pod. (Milkweed in August, and dry hard clay. Thistles the dogs brought home.)

☐

That tiny palm, pulling.

☐

Stones roll back into the sea.

Four

Words cut the throat. Scratch stone. Leave lines behind. Once incised, indelible. (Movement of the ages.) The story emerges after, not as. Fixed red.

□

I thought when I awoke I could glimpse resurrection. The sound of her singing held me. I had slept fitfully all night, listening. In another room, waves. We all listened: tide and ebb. Then murmurs. Then deep impenetrable calm. Theirs apart.

❑

If I had stayed. Braziers fanned. Battered pots. Concrete and broom. (Sweep and switch.)

❑

I hear the tap of her broom. I hear words, slow falling lines. (A falling arc.)

❑

All these things that cannot be. Colour, release, redress. (Hurry. Please! It's time.) Hand over hand. (Over mouth.) Breath. Breath. Full stop.

❑

Her voice. Mine. Her many voices. (She no come back, Joe.)

❑

Sometimes she comes back in silence, her feet padding by the door. Sometimes in a hurry, bumping and scraping. I want her there silent, curled. Waiting. Not listening. Not needing. Waiting. Outside.

❑

I do with them what I want. When I want. When I am ready. I call for them. One by one.

❑

People inhabit one room only. I would rather it stay that way. She whose house this is, who sings and sweeps. She out there, passing my door. (Bristles on wood. Slow strokes. Slow and steady and repeated.)

❑

I need not to see now. These limitations are good. Good to see just part of the valley. Good to see the window frame. In late afternoon, the room darker, the house darker, the frame darker, the aperture closing. Constriction is good. Denial is good. (Look down.)

□

High sloping, she sat askew, the arch of her thigh possible. An arching bulge, before which the stiff tongue. (Measures.) (Of music.)

□

It is something from a time before this, when water was carried in earthen jars. The opening, the belly. The dark heart.

□

Gate and stile and ditch.

❑

I could go to death like this. I could die and take this with me. (Stories go to their deaths, too.) This moment of lucidity, cradled, here. But never exactly here. Just a presence, known.

❑

(Tell me, mother, if you know now.)

❑

One line, and a bobber, and a flat stone by the inlet. All that comes by, to sea.

❑

Days pass. The rowan shore. Shells open and polished. The muscle gone.

◻

I don't know where they are today. Perhaps they have not gone away. Perhaps they are in corners, waiting. As I wait. To be invited. To something needing me.

◻

I do things that have a clear beginning and a clear ending. I eat my lunch at the table. I sweep the crumbs into the palm of my hand and deposit them in the pail. I put away the food, for tomorrow. What begins, ends. As it was. (And ever shall be.)

◻

Sparrows! (To move by flock.) One lights on the sill, quivering, surprised. I stop breathing. It carries a grain of seed, uncracked. Flickers (twice). Then it, too, gone.

□

Dry silence. (Whose voice to compare.) Dry stone, on which the water ran.

□

(Scissors and paper.) (Scissors and stone.) (Stone wins.)

□

Latin, here: an incantation. Dead words linger.

□

For choler we bleed.

□

The sharper lesson has still to be drawn. Nights spent. Focus pulled. Flesh become syllable. (Lean out. Look down.)

□

Fingering the shutter. Playing it back and forth incrementally in the groove of the hinge. Wanting more than this carefully guarded stillness.

□

I know she's there. Near the window, on the bench, leaning against the wall. I know she's there.

□

The house sounds different. Her singing is self-conscious. She drops to a hum, or stops when she moves through the room. Only at the basin, when the water slaps hard, there she sings free.

☐

I know she's there. I know where she sits. How she sits. The wall she sits against. The bench is hard. The hardness is a small pleasure. The ache of her ankle, a small pleasure. (Sometimes it starts like this.) I know her need, sudden, to move. I hear her limping, the boards creaking. I hear her crossing the room. I know when she crosses back, and when she goes into the room beside mine. I hear her lie on the bed (I hear creaking). It's then I rise and take my cup and open the door and cross quickly. My turn to move. When I return, I see her cup on the table, and sometimes a peel and a knife. Her door is open. I cross quickly, glancing quickly. I see her leg, part of it, raised on a pillow.

☐

This one I won't let speak. I can't stop her coming here. But she doesn't have to speak. She can sit there all day waiting for me to say something. I don't have to. I don't have to sit and talk to her. She can sit alone, with her book and her folded blanket. I like that, in fact, knowing she's there. Waiting, quietly, not speaking. To the others, OK. But not to me.

☐

This my ellipse. The gathering star, the far extension, the wrapping whip.

☐

I want the sill darkened wet. I want cold membrane. The slow comfort of the drip, the rising odour of the earth. (Her soil, blackening.) Here the stream of darkness, damned and rising. Taking its course.

☐

Go this step further. This more loosened. (Rent gauze, strips. Wings, flapping.)

☐

Bring the warm cup closer. Bring the edge beneath my feet. (Don't hold anything back now, Kelsey.) (I'm so lazy. Why can't I be better?) Winds picking up, sentinels nodding collusion. Knowledge of what's to come.

□

The weight and grip of it. How it rests in the grip. The whistle of it. The scent of it, peeled bare. The skin of the story, bare.

□

Over and over, this. Days of this. Slow falling lines. I breathe little. Hold little. Listen long.

□

She moves carefully, lightly, opening drawers evenly. She has closed her door. She is listening to me breathing, lying here. I hear her breathing, lying there, in the long silence, before the rustling. And the long silence again, before the stifled cry.

◻

The light at the window recedes. I have turned my chair away from the table. I am facing the wall between us, my knees at the bed. Drum tight, pulled tight. Hand-held.

◻

A breeze comes up. Lifts and settles. By listening, by memory, by mercy. Each corridor, each room, each penitential cell.

◻

I cannot hear the story, but I can imagine hearing it. (The blade catching, then prying free.)

◻

What she has before her: a clear plastic pouch, inside of which: paper, envelopes, a stick of glue. Her pen is always down. Sometimes I think she has just put it down. Sometimes she has been reading, and the book is turned over her knee. I walk quickly then, on shortened steps, the cup held out in front of me. Lest I spill a drop.

□

There is only the room I am walking through and her in it and my body moving through her vision, and my awareness of her vision, and my cup, weighing heavier and more precious, on my return. All this space, through which I alone. And she, there, watching.

□

Animal come down to drink, scenting the air. Dry brush. Dry days. Words to dust. She is there.

□

I don't know what happens next.

□

Once she knocked and I didn't answer. I didn't emerge, for hours. Took water from the kettle. Returned to my room. Crossed without looking up. Held to.

□

I used to walk the streets, late at night, listening. The thick city heat, the open windows. Leaves trembling. Breaths trembling. The sudden cry.

□

She will not go away. (Wisteria over the door.) She will sit there, in the corner, waiting. At ease in the rhythm of her days.

□

Palmful of genital, bound in cloth. Twisted. Spread. Clenched. A dance of syllables: pater ominous sanctum. This gate that has not been opened since leaves last fell. (The cress-blazoned path.) Maketh me to lie down. Luminous archèd trembling.

☐

I am the sheet, pressed upon. I am the pain I am the promise I am the given. Here, against. My unwrapped skin. My readiness.

☐

(Squalls took us. Years ago.)

☐

The measure of this, inscribed. When the body dies, the skin be salvaged. Stretched. Dried. Read.

☐

Line speaks. Line effaces. Line breaks.

☐

We met in the passageway. I stood limp, trailing. I stepped aside. In caved chest, a density of breathing. Lead cooled. Nothing moves.

☐

My body's aching. Held too long. Not the muscle tensed, but the joint contorted. (Monet's stroke.) (Deepened reds.)

☐

Still the distance across the room, still the floorboards wiped clean, the long lines of pale wood converging in the distance before her.

□

Repetition. The greedy repetition. (The green branch demanded opening.)

□

Another line across these days.

□

Some restraint is necessary. Tangent. Axis. Measure of the cell. This line goes over. Out of bounds. (On thin flesh.) I place my chair. Sit. Bare. The smooth wood. I adjust position, set angle.

□

I hear her bench scrape. She stumps over the floor. Dry profundo. I hear the washing of her cup, the gathering up. Then her door, closing.

☐

Lee pulls. Multiple lines. Discord.

☐

Sea swell. How hard it is. The tight cloth, binding. Angles open.
Heave and settle. Cave and vex. (She's breath, through caverns.
Us.)

☐

We could go on forever like this. Figures at the end of a room. I
keep seeing her there, waiting. The patience in her waiting. Her
ability to wait, to not move. Hours in her place, the warm heavy
bench, stained and rubbed smooth. I keep seeing her there, sitting,
outside her room, the light falling across her, and across the table
before her, her thighs warm. (Saplings. Green.) I keep seeing her
there, thigh over thigh, her dark wale. (Blood red.) Waiting to
begin. The story. The repetitions. Taking all of this up in her
arms. (Hyacinths. The dew.) The room spread before her in the
warm slant light. (Shafts on her flaring skin.)

■

The Lord bless us and keep us.

Five

Do you take it black? I have some milk, if you'd like.

□

The shift of one stone. A hollow disengagement. A new fixed place. A new murmur. (I don't want this.)

□

Maria says you're always making tea.

□

I don't want to keep you, if you're busy. I was just thinking of writing a letter, myself.

□

Expiration with no sound.

□

Honestly, I don't know what to say. I mean, it's such a different world out here, where do you begin? Do you know what I mean? I mean, what am I going to say, really. Dear Mom, I saw a little boy covered in flies yesterday, and they were eating the pus oozing out of his eyes. Hope you're well. Happy Birthday – ?

◻

What I know of her already. The darkness between her thighs. The roundness of her heels. The way she tenses with pleasure. (You room, too.)

◻

Hopeless against the tide.

◻

Oh, I'm all right, really. It's not broken, thank god. It's just a sprain. A bloody nasty one, as it turns out. Bloody painful. But I'll survive. There's nothing to do but wait, really. It'll heal. It just takes time, doesn't it?

◻

Pools fill. The swell of her voice. Each day, I take my place.

□

I don't mind it at all, actually. It's quite nice being an invalid for a while. I'm spoiled, really. I mean, Maria keeps an eye on me. And Sarah's such a soul. Do you know what she does? She goes down the hill first thing in the morning and brings me back fresh milk. For my tea, yes! Can you believe it? I tell her she's mad, but she won't listen.

□

To take away a mold of her thigh. To weigh its curve, the complexity of it, the warmth of it, trembling. Barely touched.

□

The shape of things matter. What is on the other side matters.

□

(The black ship rolls darkly on the sea.)

❑

You won't catch me down there again. It's bloody treacherous. I mean, it looks easy enough from up here. Those paths look a mile wide, don't they? But they're not. They're not paths, they're just little mud walls. Some of them are easy enough, they're plenty wide to walk on, really. But then all of a sudden you're stuck with no place to go but along this narrow little wall that's slippery as hell and sloping off to one side, and there's a bloody four-foot drop down to the next paddy. Well, that's what happened to me. I went right over the edge. My feet just went right out from under me and down I went.

❑

I sit at the table across from her. I hold my cup in front of me, part way across. Near my hands is a charred black circle, almost complete.

□

So there I am, soaked to the skin, bawling my eyes out.

□

Pat words. Claw caught. (In deep swells, unseen.)

□

Honestly, I thought it was broken. I thought, right, that's it, they're going to have to air evac me out of here in a helicopter and put me on a plane back home. I felt so bloody foolish. I mean, it's not like we were trekking to Everest, for god's sake. It's only a fucking rice paddy!

□

Always lifting, the long swells lifting, always under me, passing away.

◻

Do you know what he did? He crouched down and pointed for me to get on his back, and then he grabs my wrists and stands up and lifts me right up out of the muck. He carried me back to one of those wide spots, where we could all stand. Well, as soon as my foot touched the ground I let out another bloody good scream and collapsed in his arms. God, did it hurt! Poor Fernie. The man's amazing. He didn't bat an eye. He just turns around and pulls me up on his back again like a sack of potatoes and carries me all the way back up to the top of the valley. God, he was strong. And you can see for yourself I'm no feather. It must have half killed him. I swear, he was like a mule. He didn't lose his footing for an instant. Sarah says he was grinning from ear to ear when we got to the top. Proud as a peacock. All the other guides were cheering and clapping. Some cheeky bastard even took our picture, with me still hanging around Fernie's neck.

◻

Responsorye. Respondere. Respond to me. The hobbled dove. The fallen leaf. (She knows.)

◻

(Her wind-whipped hair, wet after we righted.)

☐

Well, he found a rock for me to sit on and he put me down ever so gently, but it was pretty bloody obvious I wasn't going anywhere in a hurry. And here's all these people standing around gawking at me, cracking jokes and slapping Fernie on the back. Well, I just started crying again. I couldn't help it, I completely lost it. So there's me bawling my eyes out, and there's Sarah trying to comfort me, and I'm shivering in my wet clothes, and I just wanted to die it hurt so much. So before you know it, it's Fernie again to the rescue. I swear, he hardly took a minute to catch his breath. He just threw me up on his back again, and started off down the road like he was going home for lunch. People are clapping and cheering but he didn't say a word. He just kept going all the way back here. Carried me right in the front door and plopped me down on the bed. I'm surprised you didn't hear all the ruckus.

☐

The charred circle picked at. The wood picked at. The blade point catching, then prying free. Hearts. A piercing. A ship's anchor. Viva Emile. Cintia. Terz.

◻

Many words have been spoken. Many hearts have been broken. Many wise men lied. (Forgotten, the rest.)

◻

There is nothing more than this. Words that are not mine. Old borrowed words. Pieces of something.

◻

(I see you talk him. He say you, no go. He say, careful, danger, no go.)

◻

Always this slippage. The light across her thigh. The place before me bare.

☐

Arches in the wild.

☐

Actually, it works out wonderfully for Sarah. We met this guy on the bus, on the way up here, and I think she quite fancies him. Hell of a nice guy. Only, he's got the runs, a really bad case, so he isn't going anywhere in a hurry, either. He's at the Paradise Sweet, in town. We all stayed there, the first night, but it was bloody awful. Some drunken Aussie came back late and tried to get into bed with one of the women. She was screaming blue murder. It took half the men in the place to drag him off her and throw him out. Of course, they never called the police. They never do in these places, do they? Probably just as well. The cops are no better. They'd probably have had a go at her themselves. So the next day the guy shows up at breakfast, would you believe it? He's still half pissed, and the owner lets him in! He must have been so drunk the night before he couldn't remember who he was after, and he starts checking Sarah out, right there in the middle of the dining room. You know, looking her up and down and leering at her. Well, that was it. We said, right, we've had enough of this, so we left and came up here. We figured anybody that drunk would never make it up here in the dark without falling over the edge. But Dave's still down there. That's Sarah's bloke. He's too weak to make it up here, yet. But at least he's got a private room, now, and

Sarah goes down and visits him, and takes him yogurt and crackers and things like that.

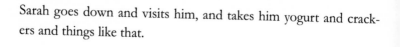

Chime, downbeat, benediction. Hers the creation, the power and the story. I am the repetition. The repeated labouring of the flesh. Lines. Accounts. Accumulations. (Forgotten, the rest.)

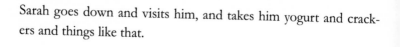

Wouldn't it be wonderful to live in a place like this? I mean, it's so quiet, all day. Back home, there's just endless traffic. Even in the middle of the night there's this dull roar. It never stops. And the worst of it is, you don't even notice it after a while. You get used to it. It isn't until you get to a place like this that you realize how mad life really is, back home. Do you know what I mean? I mean, this is the best thing that could have happened to me, in a way, being forced to stop moving for a while, and having to just sit here all day. It's like I've got the whole world to myself. I mean, I know you're in there, but honestly you're as quiet as a church mouse. Sometimes I hear your chair scrape, or the bed creak, but half the time I'm never sure if you're alive or dead. Sometimes I think I should send Maria in there to check if you're still breathing. But Maria says, no, we mustn't disturb you. She's very protective of you, you know!

□

Wrapped in her voice, held close to her side. Walking me narrower and narrower to the appointed end. Lethargy. Lethe. (Forgotten, the rest.)

□

Again this morning. Almost glimpsed. Cover of darkness. (Slipped through.) I woke and turned and it was gone. (Forgotten, the rest.)

□

Sarah says she's never met anyone she can talk to like Dave.

□

I cannot remember her face. Only her voice, and her hair falling forward, and her hand splayed and rigid on the covers.

☐

(No limit, to speak of.)

☐

I am missing words. There are not words. There is only rain, and grey arching overhead, and the hissing, swelling sea.

☐

Oh, I love a good storm. I always have. I don't know why. They scare the wits out of me, but I love them. Where I grew up we'd get these enormous storms in winter. All my little friends and me, we'd go down to the sea-front to watch. The waves were so big they'd come right over the promenade and crash onto the road. I used to love that. I used to hope they'd wash the whole bloody town away and there'd be nothing left but the cliffs and the birds and the sea. I used to face right into the wind and hold my arms out like a seagull and scream my lungs out. I'd scream "Yes! Yes!" I hated the place, it was so boring. Of course, nothing ever really happened, just a few flooded shops along the front and a sign or two knocked down by the wind. But god, I loved those storms.

What a thrill. I was so little it was all I could do to keep from getting knocked over myself. My friends would stand behind me and push me into the wind so I could get closer to the edge. And then they'd hold me there and I'd scream my lungs out. My friends thought I was half mad, but I didn't care. I loved it. The fact you could scream and scream and nobody'd take any notice of you. The whole town probably thought I was mad.

□

The drift of her voice. (She who.) The voice that turns me softer than a hand. (She who.) And each turning a momentary airing of nerves. A pulse of waiting skin.

□

(That was the best time of it, the winter storms. The shuddering rocks. The hissing, swelling sea.)

□

Along the line. Everything aligned. The sharp line drawn down the edge. Pulled tight across.

☐

(Way! Hey!)

☐

The book she's reading, always, over her knee. (Downbeat.) (Benediction.)

☐

Somewhere she is watching. She is near.

☐

There we go. A good, creamy, first cup. I always have the first cup creamy. Prepares the stomach for what's to come, me mum always says.

□

(You need this, don't you? It's what you need, isn't it?) (Não para!)

□

And that was us, really. I mean, I was shaken when it actually happened, because we just got into this argument one night, and it went on and on until it got completely out of control.

□

Veer left, veer right. The weight against my flank.

◻

Thank god we were out on the beach and not in the hostel – though I'm sure we kept the whole village awake with all our shouting. God, the things he said to me. I was shocked. I had no idea. *And* me – it wasn't just him! – I never knew I had so much venom in me. I still can't believe it, really. We went at it like a couple of alley cats. It was amazing. We never used to fight. Well, we'd bicker and argue like any couple, but never anything like that! It was horrible, really. I mean, I have to laugh at it now – what a scene! – like a bloody soap! But I mean, here we are in a foreign country – we're guests, really, aren't we? – and all these gentle, hard-working people in their houses trying to get some sleep because they have to get up before dawn and work all day, and here's Neil and I going at it full fucking throttle right on the beach, where everyone can hear us! I mean, we were screaming our lungs out. I couldn't help it. I just lost it, really – Neil too! It's a wonder we didn't come to blows. It was that close. If he'd slapped me or anything, I swear, I would have clawed his eyes out. We were shrieking at one another – and all this going on in full view of the village. You know how those villages are down south – you've been there, haven't you? – with all the houses built along the beach, just under the first line of trees? Well, there we are, standing on the beach, hurling abuse at one another at the top of our lungs – and there wasn't even a wind to drown us out. I wouldn't be surprised if they had a fiesta the next night, to celebrate us leaving town. Well, at least I did. I don't know where Neil went. These people must hate us, don't you think? I mean, we're so bloody selfish – expect them to cater to all our bloody wishes and put up with all our bloody complaints, and then we walk around with our tits hanging out like it was our own private beach and they don't even exist! I mean, just look at Maria. She works so bloody hard. Never a day off. Hardly anyone ever says thank you. Well, I mean they do, but they say it with a bloody attitude, as if it's their due, really, as if of course she's waiting on them hand and foot, and has nothing better to do with her life than wash their filthy jeans out by hand in fucking ice-cold water.

◻

Don't crack. Don't ever crack.

◻

Retract. Conceal.

◻

Somewhere in the dark the sea breaks on the shore.

◻

Sarah? No, I met her in the interior, a few days after Neil and I went ballistic.

◻

The valley beside us. The charred ring between us. The rain around us. I hold the cup to my lips, sipping at air.

◻

I was so ashamed, I just had to leave. I was so afraid I'd run into people from the hostel who'd heard me screaming. I just got on a bus the next morning and left. I went inland. I don't even remember the name of the town now. I just checked into a hotel and took a private room and cried my heart out, for days. I just went to pieces. Delayed reaction, I guess. I was so upset by what had happened. Not breaking up – I mean, I was half expecting that. I pretty much initiated it, for god's sake. And I don't think I loved him, not really. No, it was what came out of my mouth that night that upset me. Out of *my* mouth as much as his. I was just so ashamed. I still am. I can't believe it – can't believe I could be so bloody cruel. You know, when somebody does something or says something and you suddenly see a side of them you never knew existed – has that ever happened to you? Well, it was like that, but it wasn't so much Neil who shocked me – well, he did, he said some bloody awful things – but I mean, I hadn't known him that long. It's not like we'd been living together back home. – But me! Christ, it was like I was a different person – like Jekyll and fucking Hyde. Or a bloody demon in one of those exorcism movies, you know, where the kid is screaming all this filthy language and the priest says it's the devil in him. Well, that was me – I mean, the stuff that was coming out of my mouth! I still can't believe it. It was shocking, really. Absolutely vile. – Oh, god no, I couldn't. I could never – you'd never talk to me again.

☐

All these things that do not change. The light on her thigh. The blood red wale. The silence I cannot reach through. (A confusion of nests and wings. Split bark. Long shadow.)

☐

But you know what was worse? It was the things I didn't say. I mean, the things that were going through my mind, not so much while we were fighting but after. I guess I was holding something back, had some kind of civility left, though it certainly didn't feel like it at the time. But after – well, eventually we just stormed off in different directions, literally. Neil just turned his back on me and walked off in the dark, and I stormed off in the other direction, and we never saw each other again. He never came back to the hostel that night, and I took off first thing in the morning – I never even left him a note. Awful, isn't it? But the things that went through my mind after, when I was storming down the beach in a bloody rage – I must have walked for miles. I don't remember passing anyone – bloody lucky I didn't get raped – you know what those beaches are like – *and* it was the middle of the night. I don't remember anything now. I don't even remember how I got back to the hostel. All I remember are these horrible thoughts that kept running through my head – not even thoughts, really – images – my little horror films, I call them now. Bloody awful. I don't know where they came from. It still shocks me when I think of it, and I can't stop thinking of it. It's like it wasn't me – or maybe it was me, but it was a part of me I never knew was there. Do you know what I mean? And the worst of it is, once you start imagining those things – once you let yourself think them – well, it's game over. You can't erase them. It's like they move right into your head. Give them an inch and they bloody well move in. Do you know what I mean? You're not the same person anymore.

☐

The constraint of small places. Low ceilings.

□

A dead front light.

□

I replay that bloody row in my head every day. It still shocks me. You know, did I actually say those things? To Neil? Little old harmless Neil, who used to cheer me up when I got depressed about all the children begging in the streets? Ha! Well, he proved he's not so bloody harmless. I still bristle when I think of the things he said to me. The bloody cheek of him!

□

Sea run. Born blind. (The far slope in shadow.)

□

Je retourne. Je retourne.

□

For an instant I hear music. Distant chords. Open fourths. I stop
everything, stop breathing. But it stops. And again the silence. The
hissing. The rain.

□

(Lose all companions.) (Cut all ties.)

□

The placement of things matters. What is on the other side matters. (And good that way.) She sweeps past my door. She aligns the
benches with the tables and wipes the floor boards clean. I try to
hear what they say to each other, but the rain muffles everything.
Their murmurs do not last long, and then sweeping again.

□

(We must, and always. To sea again.)

◻

Whole days pass, days I do not look down. I look at the weathered planks next door, black with wet. The rain comes straight down. There is no other sound. I do not let them speak.

◻

(It was stupid of me, really.)

◻

Black rings form on the table in my room, grow darker each day. On the right, near the back. Sticky treacle. I do not wipe them clean. No one sees them, after all. Impotentia.

□

(I wanted to see how sharp. What sharp means. How deep it cuts.)

□

To keep waiting. To hold this position of waiting. To keep pressing back. Something is there.

□

(I think of the sea, the strait that lay between us, the wide expanse, the distant lights.)

□

I could go to her. There is nothing to stop me. I could have tea with her. (Talk. Tell stories.) I could invite her to my room. I could invite her to my bed. In the afternoon light I could pull closed the shutter and turn to her. I could go to her room when she lies down in the afternoon. I could sit on the bed beside her, brush my fingertips against hers, slip my palm into hers. We could talk that way, her face looking up at me, her body stretched out beside me, her eyes meeting mine.

◻

Silence is better. (Make it so I don't have to listen. Make it so she doesn't sing.) It is better this way.

◻

Descend. Decline. Diminuend.

◻

Empty and waste the sea.

◻

(You have probably heard how he went out there and didn't come back.)

◻

Bow left. Bow right. (Many a prayer.)

◻

They emerge again and again out of darkness. Beauty withered, paps dry. Detritus of past rains.

◻

I was going to knock on your door and see if you needed anything, but Maria said no, she never knocks. She said, just wait, he'll come out when he's ready.

□

Each time a word rises, and a breath, a breath rises, and a wave. Each time gathers, force gathers, each time rises, still uprise.

□

Suspended. All suspended. The falling arc suspended. (To sea! To sea!)

□

(You kill me, Joe. You kill me.)

□

Well, it's not completely better, but I can get around on it now without too much trouble.

☐

Waves claw at shingle, nudge keels.

☐

(Remember me. Remember me. Remember me.)

☐

Thrice dissolved.

☐

Streaks of colour, rising. (Here. No, here. That's better.)

◻

Make sail. Chock tiller. (Strain into the beat.) The wet sail snapping, luffing, snapping. The boom cinched in tight.

◻

No, I can't say I'm tired of it. Not yet. I just wish I could do it differently somehow – not just get on and off of buses every day, and lug my backpack around looking for a cheap place to stay. Do you know what I mean? I wish I could live here, somehow. I mean, not necessarily here, in this house or this town even, but be part of this place somehow, to feel what it's like to be them and not me for a change. And not be just another bloody tourist, getting hassled for money all the time. I mean, I know I'm being romantic. It must be awful to be poor in this country and not be able to leave and have no hope of things ever getting better. And if that's not enough, having all us bloody foreigners walking around taking pictures and flaunting our wealth and flashing our bloody tits all over the beach. But when you're just travelling and travelling and never stopping, it's like you stop seeing them as human any more. Do you know what I mean?

◻

I mean, you see some barefoot kid with open sores and flies eating the pus out of his eyes and you just about retch it hits you so hard. But the next minute someone's shoving a bunch of bananas in your face, or you've got to shove your way onto the bus before all the seats are taken, and you forget about it, don't you? I mean, you have to. You haven't got time to actually stop and register what you've seen. If you did – I mean, just stop, and just look at that kid, and feel what he's feeling, and imagine what his life is like – well, I think I'd just go to pieces on the spot. And you can't do that, not in the middle of the sidewalk with half of humanity milling about you. Besides, you know what it's like, you stop in front of one beggar and before you know it you're surrounded by all his little friends and they're all just as desperate. You've just got to keep moving. It's the only way.

□

Ducking and pitching. Birds flying low. (The arc of the striking blade.)

□

The hand moving keep the hand moving the thin circle moving limit of light.

□

Oh, I don't know. It just feels like there's something I'm not getting to, out here. I'm sure it'll hit me like a ton of bricks when I
get home to my safe little life and my job and all my friends. I
mean, at least staying here has given me that much – you know,
meeting you and Maria and our little chats, and just sleeping in the
same bed every night. And me cuppa, yes!, with fresh milk, no
less. Oh, I've had a few teary moments, when I'm alone. I haven't
gone to pieces or anything – thank god, you're probably thinking.
But, it's been good, really, feeling a little bit human again.

□

Just to say. Just to say.

□

I don't know what I'm saying, really. I just miss being close to
someone. – Neil? Oh, god no, I don't miss him! Oh, he was wonderful to me in some ways, but we were never really that close. I
never really loved him. And I don't think he loved me. In fact, I
know he didn't. He bloody well told me so, that night on the beach.

Oh, he said he loved me sometimes, but that was only to get me to go down on him. – Oh, god, I'm sorry. I'm terrible. But it's true, really. He really knew how to get to me that way. I'd do anything for him. And you know what it's like, somebody makes you feel fantastic in bed and it's got to be love, doesn't it? Well, I don't think it was, really. I mean, I know it wasn't. Not for me, anyway. We had almost nothing in common. I hated his bloody politics. I could never have married him. But I'd do anything in bed for him. He just had that magic touch. He had that power over me, and god did he use it to his advantage sometimes – the bastard! He loved it. He got exactly what he wanted, every time. I just became this other person with him. I had no shame. – Oh, god, I don't know why I'm telling you all this. I'm bloody shameless. What a slut, you must be thinking, wonder how I can get her into bed. I mean, it's not like I know you very well. But this always happens, doesn't it, when you're travelling. You spill your guts out to someone you hardly know, and then you never see them again, and you go away wondering, what was that all about? Either that, or it's the tea. Did you put something in the bloody tea?

□

(Unto us. Corpus. Body of desire.)

□

(All the nights of my life I will not release you.)

☐

Oh, it still aches a little, but I'm not worried. And Dave's such a sport. He says Sarah will carry my pack and he'll carry me, if they have to. And if I dare complain, they'll dump me by the side of the road with a tea bag and a bottle of milk and leave me for dead. Actually, I quite fancy a few days alone in a hut somewhere in the middle of nowhere, if the weather does turn rotten. You know me and storms. That's what I miss here. It's beautiful and all, don't get me wrong. I love this place. But the rain just comes straight down most of the time. It's like a sedative. It's strange, really, this past little while. I fall asleep as soon as I go to bed, and I sleep like a baby. But then I wake up suddenly in the middle of the night. I don't know what it is. It's like someone's calling me. Sometimes I lie there for hours, and I miss Neil. It's bloody awful, really. It's crazy. I hate his guts, but I miss his hands. Oh, I'll get over it. What do the Latinos say – you forget one pain by sticking a thorn in your body somewhere else? Something like that. It's only at night I miss him – and not even him, really. I mean, it's not him. Not anymore. It's something else. I don't know what it is, exactly. I can't put my finger on it. Oh, I'm probably just restless. I've been sitting around too long. I'll get over it. I'll be alright. It just takes time, doesn't it?

◻

One haunting pitch, a long note. The time of one half breath. A slow period, then silence. Then it starts again. I don't know its name, but I have heard it before. I can't say when. Enough times to remember it, when I do hear it, and to know I haven't heard it in a long time. Not here. It wasn't here. It was another room, outside another window. Always, I think of going out to look for it, but I know I will not find it. It will hear me clumsily coming and fly away.

Six

Space without sound. Only moving bodies, and darkness between. The savage stillness, the empty spaces, the long elliptical journey. But always back. Around which. Knowing she's there.

□

An area of skin delineated. Heightened colour. The effect of precision. (Here and here and here.) The rite prescribed. The sure, before the giving over. Descent into details: parts named, positions held.

◻

(Before. Always before.)

◻

The arched hollow call. The thick, inarticulate tongue. The wind-driven sleet against the pane. She leaned into it. All sidled up, beside. The steaming flank. The twitching. The muscle.

◻

(My will be done.)

◻

Many tongues, many hearts. (Forgotten, the rest.) If I. If all. And ever shall be.

■

I feel the weight upon me. The lack of a word for it. The feeling that it is all there, waiting to be taken down. The story complete, worked out in detail, ready to be born. The melody ready to be played. But it is my fingers, my clumsy fingers and my thick lulled tongue that cannot form the words and cannot make the sounds.

■

Her daily rounds, thankfully. Circle of the hours. Fire to ashes to dust.

■

I dream of a hut I will make, or find abandoned on the side of a mountain, the dirt floor dry, the thatch still good. The trees overhead sway. (Sometimes violently.) When I need sleep, I will curl on the floor.

□

A single brown fruit, still on the branch. (Gone. All gone.)

□

And each time, recollect. A bundle clutched close. Carried long, through cold thickets. Each step breaking through.

□

Bound. Shouldered. (Wrapped in her arms.) Waiting without end. There is only this waiting. World without end.

□

This a bowl. This a mound. All these things that cannot be. Wings erupt, then – absence. (My branches for the winter wren.)

❑

I listen into the silence for the sound of breathing. A mounting. An exhalation.

❑

Rings but once. Forever still.

❑

She brought me cakes this morning, on a small tray. Knocked and waited. And on it a cup of steaming water. It was the time I usually go to the kitchen. I haven't in days. Struggling to reclaim. She said nothing when I opened the door. She smiled quietly and offered the tray up, arms outstretched. I stepped back, receiving it in both hands, inhaling deeply, thanking her. I stepped back further still and turned part way into the room, opening a way for her to pass. She shook her head softly, once. Looking at me all the time. Work, she said, smiling again. Work.

◻

And so began another ritual. The tray brought to the door, with something tiny to nibble, beside the cup. The tray given and received, with tiny imperceptible bows. Intention, more than act. (The need to, acknowledged.) In such a way the room became mine again. I don't know how much she understood. She didn't try to look inside. Work. Sometimes I said it before her, and smiled and nodded, like her, and we both laughed, quietly, gentle with each other. She always turned away first. Giving me that much. Sometimes I watched her go, the shape of her body moving under her clothes, her hair lapping against her neck. (Faint lines, crossing sometimes.)

◻

I asked for the straw broom. And then, with bucket and cloth, brought back the gleam of the bare floor, and wiped clean the rings. The forest rose again from the wood. Incense of fecundity. The surface laid bare. The bedcover stretched tight.

◻

I stand beside the bed, ankles together, hands at my side, facing the window. It is night. The shutter is still open. I stand tall but slightly stooped, my head weighted forward. (It has always been this way.) The cold air rushes over my bare legs and my naked loins, and up under my shirt. This is my body.

□

The power that once flowed through me. A band, a breath, a palm settling. This was story. This was song. Wind cleansing. A ship's slow roll.

□

Sometimes it is given to us. One moment of clarity. One word laid down, cold and clattering, beside another. Ribbon of wet stone.

□

At the bottom of the breath, at the last going out, at the farthest slip back of the sea – a flutter of wings.

◻

If I can be still, and still moving. Over the last rise, through the open reach, toward the rock wall and the last high cirque. (Hawks – lifting!)

◻

The travellers gather in. Slow diminuation of their days. The folding in, the circle of voices dimming, turning in. The lost way. In deep darkness, dreams forgotten. (To chambers she led me.)

◻

As it was in the beginning. The sky we are given to lie beneath. These constellations do not reconfigure. Even the bold among us do not lie on the earth at night and imagine new beasts above us. The bear will always watch us. Hunter. And hunted.

◻

Eight cries. Four songs. The embrace all men seek. The daylight falling this way, across the arm of a deep chair. (Her good heart. Her steady days.) The reassurance of one room, closed, and a wood table, before the window. (You see, it's down there, you must lean out, look down.) These pebbles carried inland from the sea. Comfort of dry stone. We remember, too much, too poorly. We remember, none the less.

◻

One apple, quartered and cored. One piece of cheese, unwrapped. Bread, torn from a loaf. A cup, infusing.

◻

She at the faucet, soft. The water, soft. She there moving, soft. Basin to counter. (To fire.) This the miracle: the late afternoon sunlight: the stillness in her motion. And me listening. Beneath the quilt. Indolent. Redolent. Limbs free. Following the cloche of every hour. Privy to her. How she, what she. (The edges crushed soft.) She here the door open all mine listening. She here the water flowing. She here the song.

□

Not my shutter but another bangs in the night.

□

I sit in silence and one word rises, and sometimes another, sometimes in a language I do not know. Latin. Fragments. Rites I have never performed. Patter. Familia. Words rise, as if to say, I am it, I am story, and I take these words that are given (for a while they were given in dreams) and I repeat them and roll them on my tongue and carry them with me. I rub them with my fingertips, accumulations of strange words and strange sounds (because I want to, because I do whatever I want to) but they don't add up. They don't make story. They make groans in my chest and tapping on the wall. She is in there, I know, on the other side.

□

Nothing is moving in the valley. Feast days. Gone to villages, up mountain paths. (Curtains close behind them.) I have provisions. Tea. Chocolate. An extra loaf. I will wait. (A dog howls, below.) She is gone. Another girl, sullen, swabs the shower. Four days.

Three nights, maybe four. She said goodbye, asked me if I was staying. Forever, I said. We laughed. I bring fruit. My village. She stood at the open door. She know give you water. I say her. (Then) You no lonely? Long time you stay. (Then) I you friend. (Then, again) I bring fruit. My village. (Then) Gone. I closed the door. The other girl does not sing.

□

I hear my voice incanting. Words I cannot explain. Catechism. Kyrie. All manner of dead meanings. As if repetition will illuminate something. (Maketh me to lie down.) Déo. Profundus. Long tones lift on a column of air. Throat songs. Prayers. Imploring the grace of language. The words that all men know.

□

(Cold rain. And hard.)

Author's Acknowledgments

I am grateful for the encouragement and assistance of many people during the long gestation of this work. Thanks foremost to Gary Geddes, loyal and generous friend to this book and its author, and perceptive first reader. And to my sister, Sharon Gilmore, there from the beginning, example and steadying presence. My thanks also to: Judith Atkinson, Judith Cezar, Chryssa Charatsi, David Chou, Dara Culhane, William and Tekla Deverell, Geoff, Jill, Madeleine and Georgia Dodd, Emily Doolittle, Martin Duckworth and Audrey Schirmer, Ken Edwards, Ann Eriksson, Noah Eriksson and Tia Casper, Jan Geddes, Grace Gilmore and Charles Cutler, Paul and Maryke Gilmore, Jean Grant and family, Joy Green, Stephen Homer and Anne Durand, Carrie Jung, Catherine and Ken Maneker, Rob Martin, Joyce Newman, Earl and Donna Nichols, Oscar Nieto, Kathleen Oliver, Stephen Orlov and Karen Kaderavek, Harold Rhenisch, Cibele Sastre, Joanne Taylor, Betty Tully, Mariken van Nimwegan, Heidrun Voigt, and Alana Wilcox.

For time, space, and hospitality, I am grateful to The Baltic Centre for Writers and Translators, in Visby, Sweden, and The International Writers' and Translators' House, in Ventspils, Latvia. And to the Canada Council for the Arts, for travel assistance.

Parts of this book appeared for the first time in slightly different form in the journals *Great Works* (UK), edited by Peter Philpott, and *Rampike* (Canada), edited by Karl Jirgens.

This is a work of fiction. Echoes of other works, sometimes muddled, are the doing of the narrator's mind. I know he meant no harm.

JG

Other titles in Reality Street's Narrative Series

The Narrative Series has been developed out of a conviction that there is a growing body of experimental, extended prose writing which (in the UK at least) has few outlets because it doesn't fit restricted marketing categories. Titles in print so far are:

Ken Edwards: *Futures*, £9.50
Ken Edwards: *Nostalgia for Unknown Cities*, £8.50
John Hall: *Apricot Pages*, £6.50
David Miller: *The Dorothy and Benno Stories*, £7.50
Douglas Oliver: *Whisper 'Louise'*, £15
Paul Griffiths: *let me tell you*, £9

Forthcoming:
Leopold Haas: *The Raft*
Richard Makin: *Dwelling*
Sean Pemberton: *White*
Johan de Wit: *Gero Nimo*

Recent Reality Street poetry titles

Tony Baker: *In Transit*, £7.50
Ken Edwards: *eight + six*, £7.50
Allen Fisher: *Place*, £18
Jim Goar: *Seoul Bus Poems*, £7.50
Bill Griffiths: *Collected Earlier Poems*, £18
Jeff Hilson: *stretchers*, £7.50
Jeff Hilson (ed.): *The Reality Street Book of Sonnets*, £15
Allan K Horwitz/Ken Edwards (ed.): *Botsotso*, £12.50
Fanny Howe: *Emergence*, £7.50
Peter Jaeger: *Rapid Eye Movement*, £9.50
David Miller: *Spiritual Letters (I-II)*, £6.50
Wendy Mulford: *The Land Between*, £7.50
Redell Olsen: *Secure Portable Space*, £7.50
Sarah Riggs: *chain of minuscule decisions in the form of a feeling*, £7.50
Peter Riley: *Excavations*, £9
Maurice Scully: *Sonata*, £8.50
Robert Sheppard: *The Lores*, £7.50
Lawrence Upton: *Wire Sculptures*, £5
Carol Watts: *Wrack*, £7.50

Reality Street depends for its continuing existence on the Reality Street Supporters scheme. For details of how to become a Reality Street Supporter, or to be put on the mailing list for news of forthcoming publications, visit our website at: **www.realitystreet.co.uk**

Reality Street Supporters who have sponsored this book:

David Annwn
Tony Baker
Charles Bernstein & Susan Bee
Andrew Brewerton
Paul Buck
Clive Bush
John Cayley
Adrian Clarke
Lucy Clarke
Tony Cullen
Ian Davidson
Mark Dickinson
Derek Eales
Michael Finnissy
Allen Fisher/Spanner
Sarah Gall
Harry Godwin
John Goodby
Giles Goodland
Paul Griffiths
Charles Hadfield
Catherine Hales
John Hall
Alan Halsey
Robert Hampson
Randolph Healy
Jeff Hilson
Gad Hollander
Simon Howard
Fanny Howe
Peter Hughes
Elizabeth James &
Harry Gilonis
L Kiew
Peter Larkin
Sang-yeon Lee
Richard Leigh
Jow Lindsay

Tony Lopez
Chris Lord
Michael Mann
Peter Manson
Ian McMillan
Deborah Meadows
Mark Mendoza
Geraldine Monk
Maggie O'Sullivan
Richard Parker
Sean Pemberton
Pete & Lyn
Richard Price
Tom Quale
Peter Quartermain
Tom Raworth
Josh Robinson
Lou Rowan
Will Rowe
Maurice Scully
Robert Sheppard
Peterjon & Yasmin Skelt
Julius Smit
Hazel Smith
Valerie & Geoffrey Soar
Harriet Tarlo
Andrew Taylor
David Tilley
Keith Tuma
Juha Virtanen
Lawrence Upton
Catherine Wagner
Sam Ward
Carol Watts
John Welch/Many Press
John Wilkinson
Anonymous: 11